Have you heard about Epic! yet?
We're the largest digital library for kids, used by millions in homes and schools around the world. We love stories so much that we're now creating our own!

With the help of some of the best writers and illustrators in the world, we create the wildest adventures we can think of. Like a mermaid and narwhal who solve mysteries. Or a pet made out of slime.

We hope you have as much fun reading our books as we had making them!

For my grandmothers

—C.S.

For my niece, Sydney

—R.K.

epic!

My Pet Slime

Courtney Sheinmel
Illustrated by Renée Kurilla

Andrews McMeel
PUBLISHING®

1

Show and Tell

School was just okay today.
After lunch, our teacher, Ms. Serrato,
called on Table A to do Show and Tell.
There's a girl in my class named Claire
who says Show and Tell is a little kid
thing to do. We had it in kindergarten.
But it stopped when we got to first grade,

and we didn't do it in second grade, either. Which just proves, according to Claire, that third grade is WAY too old for it.

Claire is really popular. Kids always agree with her. Out loud, I agree with her, too. Life is easier when you agree with Claire.

But here's the truth: I secretly think that Claire is wrong about Show and Tell. Sure, little kids do it. But little kids do lots of things that older kids do. Like . . .

- **They eat ice cream.**
- **They dangle their legs in the pool.**
- **They do art projects.**

Speaking of art projects, I do A LOT of them. I'm practicing so that when I grow up, I'll be as good as Frida Kahlo, and Leonardo da Vinci, and Michelangelo. Their artwork is in museums all over the world.

I want MY artwork to be in museums one day, too. Then Claire and everyone else will see my name in big letters on a shiny gold plaque.

Piper Maclane

But that's not the subject right now. The subject is Show and Tell, and how I really *do* like it, even though I don't admit that out loud.

Except today I didn't like it so much. My friend Benny was the last person to share. He passed around a picture of his hamster. He told us some hamster facts. Like . . .

- **Hamsters are very friendly.**
- **They store food in their cheeks to eat later.**
- **They need a lot of exercise, so it's good to put a wheel in their habitats.**

Another thing about hamsters is that I'm allergic to them. I'm also allergic to dogs, cats, rabbits, guinea pigs, gerbils, chinchillas . . .

The list goes on and on. If it's cute and cuddly, then my eyes get teary and I can't stop sneezing.

I'm NOT allergic to lizards, or frogs, or our class pet, Mr. Swimmers, who's an angelfish. But I want a pet that can sleep in my bed with me at night. Not the kind that has to sleep in a tank.

Benny was really happy about his hamster. I know I should be happy for him. But it's hard to be happy for someone when they have something that you want but you can't have—even if that someone is your friend.

"Does the hamster have
a name?" Ms. Serrato asked.
"Yep," Benny said.

Show and Tell

"It's Ty. Short for Tyrannosaurus Rex. I wanted him to have a big name because he's such a little guy."

"That's very thoughtful," Ms. Serrato said.

"Why don't you call him Rex?" Claire called out.

"Because I call him Ty," Benny said.

"I think it should be Rex," Claire said.

"Me too," Eleanor said.

"Me three," Beatrice said.

See how everyone agrees with Claire?

"Well . . . " Benny said.

I could tell even Benny wanted to agree with her . . . but he *didn't* want to change his pet's name.

"Does anyone else have any questions?" Ms. Serrato asked.

Theo raised his hand.

"Yes, Theo?" Ms. Serrato said.

"I have a cat named Charlie," Theo said.

"I have a rabbit named Cinnabunny," Diego said.

"I have three mice named Eeny, Miney, and Moe," Izzy said.

"OMG, I have the best idea," Claire said.

OMG means Oh My Goodness, in case you don't know.

"This whole week should be *pet* Show and Tell week," Claire said. "Tomorrow,

I'll bring in a picture of my dog, Buddy, and tell you about all the tricks he knows. Everyone else at Table B—bring pictures of *your* pets, too."

"These are comments, not questions," Ms. Serrato said.

"I have a question," I said.

"Yes, Piper?"

"What if you're at Table B, but you don't have a pet?"

"Everyone has a pet," Beatrice said. "Because we all have Mr. Swimmers."

"Anyone is welcome to bring whatever they want, okay, Piper?" said Ms. Serrato.

"Okay," I said.

"All right," Ms. Serrato said. "Thank you, Benny. You may sit down now. And thank you, Table A. Table B, you're on for tomorrow."

Slime Time

After school, Dad picked me up. Some afternoons, Dad and I do things together, like going to the park or making homemade ice cream.

But today, Dad said that he hadn't finished his words yet, so I needed to play quietly by myself.

Dad writes books. Every day, he makes himself write a certain number of words before he's finished with work for the day. We have an extra bedroom in our house that Dad uses as an office. My mom is a lawyer. She doesn't have an office in our house. She has an office in a building, along with a lot of other people.

I did my homework while Dad wrote his words. When I was done, I knocked on his office door.

"Yes?" he called.

I pushed the door open. "I'm all done with my homework," I said.

"I wish I was all done with my work," Dad said.

"How many words do you have left?" I asked.

"Why?"

"Because if you don't have many, you'll get to stop soon, and we can play something together."

"Sometimes even a few words can take a long time to write when I'm working on a difficult section," Dad said. "You'll have to play on your own today, okay?"

"Okay," I said.

I was feeling sad again—not because Dad still had work, but because of my allergies. If I wasn't allergic, I could have a pet, and I'd never have to play alone.

But allergies = NO pets.

I decided to do an art project, because art always cheers me up.

Different artists use different materials for their work. Like:

- **Claude Monet used oil paints.**
- **Auguste Rodin used clay.**
- **Annie Leibovitz is a photographer, so she uses a camera.**

As for me, I like to work with slime.

Yep, you read that right: slime.

Slime is the very best material of all. You can do so many different things with it—stretch it, braid it, loop it, sculpt it.

Unfortunately, I didn't have any fresh slime to work with.

But I did have all the ingredients to make a new batch.

Technically, I'm not supposed to make slime without Mom or Dad there to supervise. I thought about knocking on Dad's office door again. But I knew he still had work to do, so he probably wouldn't help.

Besides, I didn't need his help. I've made slime with Mom and Dad so many times, and I know exactly what to do. You only need three ingredients:

1. Glue

2. Baking soda

3. Mom's contact lens solution

 Oh, and one more ingredient: food coloring. You don't *need* it to make the slime. But slime is really plain-looking without it. It's like the color of a piece of drawing paper or a white T-shirt.

I gathered everything up, along with a measuring cup and a bowl, and headed into my room. My stuffed animals were lined up on my bed.

Claire probably thinks stuffed animals are babyish, too. But she's wrong again. They're cute and cuddly, and you can have so many different species without being allergic to any of them.

"What time is it?" I asked my stuffed animals. They didn't answer, but I answered for them: "It's SLIME TIME!"

First, I squirted out the glue, then added the baking soda and the contact lens stuff. I'd forgotten a spoon, but that was okay. I mushed everything together with my hands, and PRESTO!

Fresh slime!

I spent a few more minutes mushing it around. I love the feeling of slime. It's so soft and squishy. It's too bad there isn't a pet that has slime for fur. That would definitely be the perfect pet for me.

Hmm . . . what would my perfect slime pet look like?

19

Well, first of all, it would be purple, because purple is my favorite color. I pulled off a big hunk of slime and squeezed in a drop of red food coloring and then a drop of blue. I mushed it all together, and *voila*! I had a blob of purple slime. I shaped it into a kitten-size animal, but my slime pet was too round to really be a kitten. I gave it big eyes, a little mouth, and two arms that were on the small side, but still long enough for hugs.

Oh, it was so cute. Cute and perfect. Well, not quite perfect.

Perfect pets are alive. They roll over, play fetch, and lick your face with kisses. Slime pets can't do any of that.

"I wish you were real," I said, patting my pet's slimy head.

"If you were real, you'd be as friendly as Benny's hamster, and do tricks like Claire's dog. But you're just . . . slime."

"Hey, Piper!" Dad called. "I'm all finished!"

I heard his footsteps coming up the hallway toward my room. The problem was, my room looked kind of messy.

Okay, fine. It looked VERY messy.

I couldn't let Dad come inside. I ran to the door and opened it just as he got there. "Hey, what's going on?" he asked.

"Uh, nothing," I said. "Absolutely, positively nothing."

"Hmm," he said. He tried to peek inside.

"No, don't," I said. "I'm trying to . . . I'm trying to clean it up."

"Oh, really?"

"Yeah," I said. "I'm in the mood to clean. I'm actually going to get the vacuum cleaner."

"Do you want my help?" Dad asked.

"Nope. I want to do it all by myself."

"All right, then," he said. "You do that, and I'll get started on dinner."

Surprise, Surprise

Here's something that shouldn't be true, but it is: It's always way easier to make a mess than to clean it up.

You'd think it'd be about the same. But it's not. Before I was even half-finished cleaning, I heard Dad calling me again. "Piper, come here!

Mom's home, and she has a surprise guest with her!"

I love surprise guests. And I really, really wanted it to be a certain surprise guest.

"See you later," I told my slime pet, and I ran out of my room.

I didn't want to get my hopes up, because the surprise guest could've been anyone, like one of Mom's work colleagues. They're mostly nice, but also mostly boring.

The surprise guest I wanted it to be is the opposite of boring, and my hopes were already up about it being her. That's the thing about your hopes—they go up all on their own. You can't stop them.

And luckily, it was just who I wanted. "Grandma Sadie!" I cried.

"Pipsqueak!"

Grandma Sadie lives an hour away from us, which isn't really that far. But she travels a lot for her job, so we don't get to see her much at all.

She doesn't have a regular job, by the way. She works for AstroBlast Explorers! I'm sure you've heard about it, because it's very famous. But just in case you haven't, the job of an AstroBlast Explorer is to explore things—obviously.

In the old days, there were people who explored the different parts of the earth. The AstroBlast Explorers explore things in space!

I gave Grandma Sadie a big hug. "I thought you weren't coming back for six more *months*!"

"I had an unexpected trip home for a couple of days," Grandma Sadie said.

"Is this your 'wow' for the day?" Dad asked me. Every day, Dad asks me about my wow and pow—wow means the best thing that happened to you all day, and pow means the worst thing.

"Oh, yes!" I said. "Grandma Sadie is such a big wow, I don't even remember my pow."

"You want to see the surprise I brought you?" Grandma Sadie asked.

"Yes, please," I said.

"Oh, Mother," Mom said. "You don't need to bring Piper a present *every* time you visit. Your presence is present enough. Right, Pipe?"

"Yes, of course," I said—and I meant it, but . . .

As long as Grandma Sadie had already brought a present, I should get to see it, right?

Grandma Sadie's presents were always unusual. She didn't knit me sweaters or sneak me candy, like other kids' grandmas. Not even close.

Instead, one time she gave me a package of special space meals: spaghetti and meatballs and ice cream sandwiches. They came in plastic bags with all the air sucked out of them. Another time, she brought me a weird black rock with swirls in it. It was made of lava—from Mars!

29

"Piper, go fetch my bag," Grandma Sadie said. "It's by the front door."

"Coming right up!" I said.

I ran to the front door. Grandma Sadie's bag was big and shiny, like a pillow covered in aluminum foil. It was heavy, too. I half-carried, half-dragged it back to her.

"Thank you, Pipsqueak," Grandma Sadie said. She snapped it open and mumbled as she dug around inside. "Let's see . . . let's see . . . "

I was so excited. I felt my heart starting to beat harder. Would I get a comet rock? Or a drop of diamond-rain from Jupiter? Or maybe a piece of Saturn's ring?

Whatever it was, it was definitely coming with me to Show and Tell tomorrow!

"Here!" Grandma Sadie said.

She held the present out to me.

Space Dust

Grandma Sadie handed me a small plastic bottle. The see-through kind that medicine comes in. But there wasn't medicine in this bottle. Instead, there was . . .

Well, it looked like there wasn't anything at all.

"Do you like it?" Grandma Sadie asked.

"Um . . . I can't tell what it is."

"It's space dust collected from around the cosmos," she said.

"What's the cosmos?"

"The universe."

"Oh," I said, and I started to unscrew the top.

"Don't do that, dear. You don't want to make a mess."

How could I make a mess with something that was practically invisible?

"Don't worry," Dad said. "Piper's been practicing with the vacuum cleaner."

Mom raised an eyebrow.

"I think it's better to keep it in the bottle for the time being," Grandma Sadie said. "All right, Pipsqueak?"

"All right," I said. I rocked the bottle from side to side and squinted to see the dust. "We have Show and Tell

34

tomorrow. I'd bring this in, but you can't tell there's anything in there. If I say it's space dust, Claire will think I made it up. Do you have something else I could bring?"

"That's all I brought back," Grandma Sadie said. "I'm sorry."

"It's okay," I said.

"Piper, I think you're forgetting a couple more words," Mom said.

"Oh, right. Thank you."

"You're welcome, Pipsqueak," Grandma Sadie said.

"I don't know about you guys," Dad said. "But I'm pretty hungry. Anyone else want dinner?"

"I do," Grandma Sadie said. "Traveling home from the space station always makes me famished."

"Great. Turkey burgers coming right up."

He brought a platter of burgers to the table with all the fixings, plus sweet potato fries on the side. Mom started asking Grandma Sadie about her work. "Where'd you just come back from?"

"I'm afraid I can't say," Grandma Sadie said.

"What are you working on?"

Grandma Sadie shook her head. "Can't say that either."

Conversations with Grandma Sadie always go like this. The people at AstroBlast Explorers work on a lot of super-secret things.

"Do you want to stay over tonight, Mother?" Mom asked. "Piper could sleep in Tom's office, and you could take her bed."

Uh oh.

I wouldn't mind giving up my bed for Grandma Sadie . . . but my room wasn't exactly clean enough for her to sleep in there.

"Thanks, dear," Grandma Sadie said to Mom. "But I need to get home tonight to pack. The AstroBlast Explorers are going on a trip tomorrow."

Phew.

"Where are you headed this time?" Dad asked.

Grandma Sadie smiled, and I knew what she was going to say: "I'm afraid I can't say."

"Can't blame a guy for asking," Dad said.

When dinner was over, Mom drove Grandma Sadie back to the train station, and I helped Dad with the dishes.

"Hey, Piper," Dad said. "Why don't you log on to my computer and write Grandma Sadie a little thank you email?"

"I told her thank you," I reminded him.

"I know, but I'm not sure she knew that you meant it."

"Well, dust is just . . . dust."

Dad shook his head, and I knew he was disappointed in me. "In this house, it's the thought behind a gift that counts, not the gift itself.

"Grandma Sadie always thinks of you, and you should be thankful for that."

"Okay, okay," I said. "I'll write to her."

I headed into Dad's office and sat down at his desk.

Dear Grandma Sadie,

I know it's the thought that counts, so thank you for thinking of me. It's nice to have space dust. If you see anything cooler than dust the next time you're in space, can you bring me some? (But if you can't, that's okay, too.)

Love, Piper

41

DID YOU HEAR SOMETHING?

After that, I went to my room to get ready for bed. My slime pet was still on my desk. Actually, he looked more like a blob than a pet. His little mouth and arms had melted into his blobness. I fixed them up. "There you go," I said.

I changed into my PJs. Mom knocked on the door to say goodnight, and I forgot to tell her not to come in.

"Oh my goodness. What happened in here?" she asked.

"What do you mean?"

"Oh, come on now, Piper," Mom said. "I know you know what I'm talking about."

"I made a little bit of slime," I admitted.

"By yourself?"

"Yes."

"In your *room*?"

"Yes."

"You know better than that," Mom said. "You're not allowed to make slime

43

without Dad or me supervising, and all slime-making is supposed to take place in the kitchen."

"I knew about the first rule," I said. "I didn't know the second one."

"The second rule is one you should've realized without needing to hear it," Mom said. "There's slime sticking to everything in here, even the walls. How'd you manage to get it on the *walls,* Piper?"

"I don't know," I said. "But don't worry. Slime peels off. Watch."

I tugged on a string of slime that was stuck to the wallpaper. It came right off . . . except for a little bit. I scratched the leftover slime with my nail. There. You couldn't tell it'd ever been there.

Well, you *mostly* couldn't tell.

"I'm sorry," I said.

"What were you thinking, Piper?"

I shrugged. "I don't know," I said. "I felt bad when I got home from school because Benny got a pet hamster, and I can't have one. And I can't have a dog like Claire and Beatrice, or a cat like Theo, or a rabbit like Diego, or mice like Izzy, either."

"Mice?" Mom said. "You want a pet mouse now?"

"I want a pet *something*," I said. "But I'm allergic to *everything*. Except for slime. So, I decided to make my own slime pet. That's him, on my desk. He was cute when I first made him—the size of a kitten, but rounder, with big eyes and a little mouth, plus arms for cuddling. You can't tell now. That's the problem with a slime pet—it doesn't keep its shape. Well, the *second* problem. The first problem is that it's not alive."

"I see," Mom said.

"Am I going to be punished?" I asked.

"Yes, I'm afraid so," Mom said. "When you get home from school tomorrow, the first thing you have to do is clean your room. And even after you're finished cleaning, there won't be any more slime-making in this house for the rest of the—"

"Day?" I filled in.

"Week," Mom said.

"A week? But Mom, that's way too much time!"

"We'll see what kind of cleaning job you do and discuss it again tomorrow. Come on, get into bed. I'll tuck you in."

I climbed into bed. Mom stepped toward me, but she stopped to pick something up from the floor. "What's this?" she asked, holding out the bottle from Grandma Sadie.

"It must've rolled out of my pocket when I changed into my PJs," I said.

"I'm putting it right here on your bookshelf, okay?"

"Okay."

"Sweet dreams, Piper," Mom said. She leaned down to kiss me goodnight. Then she headed for the door.

"Mom?"

"Yes?"

"I'm sorry I broke the rules. And I'm not just saying that to get out of a punishment. I really am sorry."

"I know you are. I'll help you clean up tomorrow. Go to sleep now, okay?"

"Okay," I said.

She switched off the light.

I snuggled under the covers, trying to get cozy. If I had a pet in bed with me, it'd be easier. But I found a good, warm spot and closed my eyes.

That's when I heard the sound.

IT'S ALIVE!

It was a rumbling sound, kind of like the one your stomach makes when you're feeling hungry.

But I wasn't hungry, and the sound wasn't coming from my stomach or any of my other organs. It wasn't coming from me at all.

Who was it coming from? I was alone in my room . . . at least, I was *supposed* to be.

My heart started to pound. I clutched my covers close and looked around. It was dark, but there was a little bit of light coming in through the slats of the blinds. I could see the shapes of things. My bookshelves, my desk chair, my desk . . .

Oh no, what was that on my desk? My heart pounded even harder.

But then I remembered my slime pet. That's all it was.

Phew.

The room was quiet again. Maybe I'd imagined the rumble. Maybe it was part of a dream. I didn't *think* I'd been dreaming, but that can happen sometimes. Right when you're between being awake and asleep, you can confuse what's real and what you made up in your head.

I let my eyes close again.

Rumble. Rumble. Rumble.

My eyelids flicked back open. That was definitely NOT a dream. A breeze blew through the window. Something fell off my bookshelf and onto the floor. It rolled over to the foot of my bed.

I was ready to scream for Mom or Dad if I had to. But first, I peeked over the edge of the bed to see what had fallen. It was the bottle of dust from Grandma

Sadie. Mom must've put it too close to the
edge, and the wind knocked it over. Okay.
That was NBD, as Claire would say.

NBD means No Big Deal.

I almost left the bottle there, because
my bed felt warm and cozy. But then

I realized that I might not remember it was there in the morning. I didn't want to accidentally step on it. I crawled out from under the covers and reached down to pick it up.

The bottle felt warm in my hands, like someone else had been holding it, and the warmth from their hands was on the bottle. I squinted to try and see the dust. It looked like nothing.

No, that wasn't true. Not anymore. Now it looked like it was sort of glowing.

My hand that was holding the bottle started to glow a little bit, too.

The bottle rumbled in my hand.

I *knew* I'd heard something. I knew it!

You'd think I'd start to feel scared again. But I didn't feel scared. I heard a voice say, *Open me.*

It wasn't an out-loud voice. It was more like a voice in my head. But I listened to it anyway and started to unscrew the top.

Then I heard Grandma Sadie's voice: *Don't do that, dear.*

I stopped unscrewing.

But Grandma Sadie had only been worried about the dust being messy, and I'd be careful not to make a mess.

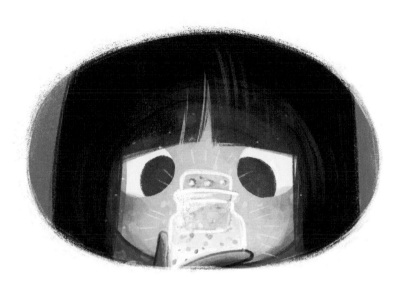

My fingers were itching to open the bottle, so I did.

A beam of light shot out of the top of the bottle. The dust was glowing and swirling around. I guess I wasn't holding the bottle tightly enough, because it jumped out of my hands.

That's right—the bottle jumped! I didn't know bottles could do that!

The swirly dust flew out the top and landed on my slime pet. It sparkled for a few seconds before fading back to nothing. The empty bottle rolled onto the floor. I picked it up and put it on my desk—far back enough that it wouldn't fall off again.

But jumping bottles can jump even if you put them far back, so that wasn't good enough. I shut it in the top drawer. There—now it wouldn't go anywhere.

"You okay?" I asked my slime pet.

He didn't answer. He looked fine, though. You couldn't see what color he was, because my room was too dark. You couldn't see what shape he was,

either. But that wasn't the dark's fault—
he'd melted back into a slime blob again.

Right when I was going to turn
around and get back into bed, the
rumbling sound started again.

This time, it was coming from
the slime!

My breath caught in my throat.
I felt my eyes getting bigger and bigger
and bigger as I watched my slime pet.

First, it started to glow. Then
it started to sparkle. And then—
you're never going to believe this—
the blob of slime started sculpting itself
back into the shape I'd made it! Its little
arms grew back, and it blinked open

its eyes. Its mouth popped up and started twitching.

"Ah, ah, ah . . . " it said, squeezing its eyes shut.

I squeezed my eyes shut, too. *When I open my eyes*, I told myself, *everything will be normal again. The slime will be back to a blob.* I opened my eyes.

" . . . choo!" the slime pet sneezed.

"Mom!" I screamed. "Dad! Come in here!"

Mom rushed in. "Piper, what's wrong?" she asked.

I pointed to the slime pet on my desk. "It's alive!" I said.

STILL THERE

"What's alive?" Dad asked, coming in behind Mom. He flicked on the lights. There were little bits of purple slime on the carpet. "What happened in here? Piper, did you make *slime* in your *room*?"

"She did it after school when you were working," Mom told him.

"Oh, Piper," Dad said. "You know making slime by yourself in your room is not allowed."

"I covered this with her earlier, Tom," Mom said. "What I don't understand is how this room got even *messier* since I left it!"

"It's not my fault," I said. "The slime turned alive and it sneezed. That's slime SNOT all over the floor!"

"Ah," Dad said. "It sounds like someone had a bad dream."

"I wasn't dreaming," I insisted. "It happened. I swear. I—"

I looked over at my slime pet. He was back to a slime *blob*.

"Come on, Pipe," Mom said. "Let's get back into bed."

"It happened," I said. "It really did."

"I'll rub your back for a few minutes, okay?" she said.

"Okay."

I got back into bed. Dad called goodnight from the doorway and switched off the lights. Mom started to rub my back. "There, there," she said. "There, there." I closed my eyes, and that's the last thing I heard before I fell asleep.

When I woke up in the morning, I didn't remember everything right away.

I like to stretch out my body before I open my eyes. First my arms, then my legs. My foot slipped under something warm at the end of my bed.
Maybe it was a pillow, or one of my stuffed animals. It felt extra cozy.

I opened my eyes and looked down. There, at the end of my bed, my slime pet was looking right at me.

I squeezed my eyes shut tight and tried opening them again.

He was still there.

I had to be dreaming. I just had to be.

I pinched myself hard on the arm.

"Ow!"

Nope, not dreaming. My slime pet was *still* there, looking back at me.

He was real. He was alive. I'd made him and wished that he could be real. And now, he *was*.

I patted the bed right next to me. "Come here," I said.

"Piper! Time to get up!" Dad called.

His voice sounded very far away. The only thing I could concentrate on was my slime pet. It crawled toward me and curled up next to me.

"Hi, little one," I said.

He gurgled and rumbled, like he was saying "hi" back to me.

"My name is Piper," I said. "I'm your pet mom. This is my room, so it's your room, too. Do you like it?"

More gurgles.

"You know what? You need a name. How about Cooper? No, you don't look like a Cooper. Maybe . . . Tucker? I don't think you're a Tucker, either. Hmm . . . how about . . . how about Cosmo? Because Grandma Sadie said the dust came from the cosmos. And the word 'cosmos' sounds kind of like 'cozy.' What do you think, Cosmo? Do you like your name?"

He gurgled some more and wrapped his teeny tiny arms around mine. "That is the coziest hug!" I said, squeezing him back. "Oh, Cosmo, we're going to have so much fun together. We'll play fetch and cuddle up at night, and I'll teach you tricks just like Claire taught Buddy."

Cosmo looked up at me, like he was waiting for me to teach him something.

"You want your first lesson now, do you? Okay. I'll teach you how to sit. Sit, Cosmo. Sit."

Cosmo didn't move.

"Sit, Cosmo," I said, and I pushed down gently on his slimy little butt. Cosmo sat, but when I moved my hand, his butt popped back up. "I guess it's going to take some practice," I said.

"Piper, didn't you hear Dad calling you?" Mom said. She pushed open my door before I even had a chance to answer.

"Mom! Mom! Look at this!"

"Why is the slime on your *bed*?"

"I told you it was alive!" I cried. I'd looked up when Mom walked into the room. But now I looked back down at my slime pet.

Only, it wasn't a pet at all anymore. It was just a slime blob.

"Oh, Cosmo!" I said.

"Oh, *Piper*," Mom said.

"Wait." I blinked a bunch of times and pinched myself again. But it was no use. Cosmo was nothing but a blob. "I don't know what happened."

"It's clear to me what happened," Mom said.

"What?"

"You got out of bed, picked the slime up from your desk, and brought it back into bed with you. The question is WHY— why would you do that? It's going to get all over your sheets."

"I didn't do it," I said.

"Piper—"

"I'm telling you the truth," I said. "The slime turns alive when you're not here. It has something to do with Grandma Sadie's space dust. The bottle fell on the floor last night, so I picked it up and opened it—"

"Grandma Sadie told you *not* to open it," Mom said.

"I *had* to open the bottle," I said. "It was rumbling and glowing. But when I unscrewed the top, the dust shot out and landed on Cosmo."

"Cosmo is the slime, I presume?"

"Yes! And then he turned alive! It was like magic!"

"You're a very good storyteller," Mom said. "Maybe one day, you'll write books like your dad does. But right now, you need to get ready for school. And this—"

She stepped forward and reached for Cosmo. "Be careful," I said. "I don't want you to hurt him."

"It's just slime," Mom said. "I'm putting it on your desk. We'll deal with the cleanup—and punishment—when you get home from school."

She looked at her watch.

"Shoot—I'm running late for a meeting. Your dad is making breakfast. Do I have to stand here and make sure you get dressed, or can I trust you to do it on your own?"

"You can trust me," I said. "Have a good day at work."

"Have a good day at school," she said. "I love you, even if you're taking this slime thing a little too far."

"Love you, too."

She gave me a quick peck on the cheek and walked out of the room.

I looked over at Cosmo. Would he wake up again? Would he stay a blob forever?

He blinked open his eyes and smiled up at me.

BACK TO SCHOOL

"Here you go, Piper," Dad said. He scooped some scrambled eggs onto a plate.

"Thanks." I put my backpack on the floor by my feet extra gently.

"Whoa, you've got a lot of stuff in there," Dad said.

"I . . . uh . . . I made a project for school," I told him.

It wasn't really a school project. It was Cosmo. I'd put him into my backpack, along with a small blankie, so he'd feel all cozy. I'd also cut a few small holes in my backpack. I hoped Dad wouldn't notice them. I didn't have any choice. I couldn't leave Cosmo home alone, so I needed something to carry him in— something with breathing holes.

"Orange juice?" Dad asked.

"Yes, please."

He turned around. I bent down, unzipped my backpack a little bit, and rubbed the top of Cosmo's little head.

"Here you go," Dad said, placing a glass of juice in front of me. I felt Cosmo's body under my hand, turning from something alive back to regular slime.

I was starting to understand the magic, sort of—as long as I was the only one close enough to Cosmo to see him, he turned alive. But when Mom or Dad showed up, he turned back into a plain old slime blob.

"We're running late," Dad said. "You've only got four minutes to eat before we have to go."

When I finished, Dad handed me my lunchbox. He turned to rinse the dishes in the sink, and I unzipped my backpack again. "Hey," I whispered to Cosmo. "Sorry, I know it's getting tight in there."

I stuffed my lunchbox behind the blankie. Dad turned off the sink. As I zipped up my backpack, I saw that Cosmo was a blob again.

"Grab your raincoat," Dad said. "It's supposed to rain today."

It wasn't raining yet, and we speed-walked to school. Speed-walking is easier for Dad, because his legs are longer. I had to jog a little to keep up. Then I worried that Cosmo was bumping around too much, so I kept swinging my backpack forward and peeking inside.

With Dad right there next to me, Cosmo was as blobbish as ever.

"Is that too heavy?" Dad asked. "I can carry it for you."

"No, thanks," I said.

By the time we got to school, Ms. Serrato was already at the front of the room, getting ready to teach. I rushed to my seat.

"Put your backpack in your cubby, Piper," she said.

"I don't mind keeping it by my seat," I said. I *wanted* to keep it by my seat, so I could keep peeking in on Cosmo.

"Backpacks belong in cubbies," Ms. Serrato said. "As soon as you put your stuff away, we can get started."

Everyone was watching me as I walked to the back of the room. My cubby was the second from the end on

the left. I hung my backpack on the peg and unzipped it to get my homework folder—and also to check on Cosmo. No one could see him, because I was standing in a way that blocked the view. He looked up at me with his big, dark eyes. I knew he wanted to climb out and play. But if he climbed out, he'd just be a slime blob. And if he was a slime blob, people might poke him or stretch him or hurt him.

"Sit, Cosmo," I whispered, and I pushed down on his slimy little butt. "Good boy," I said softly.

"Piper?" Ms. Serrato called.

I zipped up my backpack and returned to my seat.

84

Ms. Serrato said we would start the day with math. She turned around to write on the board, and I twisted in my chair to look over at my backpack. It was just hanging there in my cubby. How was Cosmo doing inside? Was he getting enough air?

"Piper, do you have the answer for this one?" Ms. Serrato asked.

I whipped back around. "What?"

"Number three on your worksheet," she said. "Do you have the answer?"

"Uh . . . four hundred and seventeen."

"Good."

She turned back to the board, and I snuck another look.

Once math was over, it was time for geography. While everyone switched books, I went to check on Cosmo and give him a few pets. I checked on him again when geography was over, and we were moving on to our Spanish lesson.

"Why do you keep going back there?" Claire asked, once I'd returned to my seat.

"No reason," I said.

"There's got to be a reason," she said. "You have something in your backpack, don't you?"

"I—"

"Girls," Ms. Serrato said. "Do you have anything to share with the class?"

That's what she always says when she catches people whispering during class time. I shook my head.

"No," I told her. At the same time Claire said, "Piper has been getting up to check her backpack A LOT."

"I don't think that's any of your concern, Claire," Ms. Serrato said.

I nodded, because Ms. Serrato was right. It *wasn't* Claire's concern.

Then she added, "Stay in your seat, Piper."

But after Spanish, it was time for lunch, and everyone left their seats to get their lunchboxes. I went to my cubby and picked up my backpack. My plan was to take it to the cafeteria with me.

Ms. Serrato stopped me. "You can leave that in your cubby," she said.

"My lunchbox is in it."

"Take your lunchbox out."

"I have something important in my backpack," I said.

"I knew it!" Claire said. "Is it for Show and Tell?"

"Um . . . maybe."

"Piper," Ms. Serrato said. "I understand wanting to keep important things close. But whatever it is, it's safer to leave it here in the classroom than to take it to the cafeteria and the playground. It won't get lost if you leave it right here. Okay?"

"Okay," I said.

I put my backpack back in my cubby. Claire was standing soooo close. I knew she wanted to peek inside.

I blocked her view as I unzipped it to take out my lunchbox and gave Cosmo a couple of goodbye pats.

When I zipped my backpack up again, I left it about this much open:

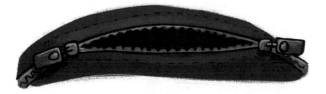

Big enough so if Cosmo needed a bit more air, he could stick his teeny mouth out.

"Bye," I said softly.

"Did you just say 'bye' to your backpack?" Claire asked.

"No," I said.

Technically it wasn't a lie. I didn't say "bye" to my backpack. I said it to something *inside* my backpack.

"Okay, Class 3B," Ms. Serrato said. "Let's head out!"

LOST

I was thinking about Cosmo when I flipped open my lunchbox. Claire leaned over. "Whatcha got?" she asked.

I shook my head. "Nothing," I said.

I'd never had nothing in my lunchbox before.

"Your parents didn't give you anything to eat?" Claire said. "Whoa. *My* parents would never do that."

"My parents would never do it either," I said. "At least not on purpose. My dad must've thought my mom made my lunch, and my mom must've thought my dad did. Do you have anything you can trade?"

"Sure," she said.

"Really?"

"JK!"

JK means Just Kidding.

A few of the other kids at the table started laughing. Eleanor gave Claire a high-five.

"I only trade when the other person has something good," Claire said. "And you don't have anything at all."

She was right. My stomach growled. I was hungry, and I knew I'd only get hungrier and hungrier until it was time to go home.

"You can have half my sandwich," Benny said.

"Wow. Thanks," I said.

"Here, have a Twizzler, too."

"I'll pay you back in Oreos tomorrow," I told him. "When my mom packs lunch, she gives me two, but sometimes my dad gives me three—and I'll give them all to you."

"That's okay," he said. "You don't have to."

By the time we finished eating, it had started to rain, so we had indoor recess. A lot of kids don't like indoor recess. But I think it's pretty fun. You get a choice of playing board games, doing art projects, or just talking to your friends.

I always pick art. Even though school doesn't have any slime-making projects, I can draw things to sculpt from slime when I get home.

Except today I was being punished, so I wouldn't be allowed to make slime for sculpting. Besides, I was worried about the slime I'd already made. Poor little Cosmo was all alone in Ms. Serrato's classroom. I had to go check on him. I couldn't wait until the end of recess. But there was a problem.

Actually, two problems.

1. Mr. Berry

2. Mrs. Fisher

Mr. Berry and Mrs. Fisher are the lunch aides. When we have indoor recess, they stand by the big doors at the end of the lunchroom like they're the guards of us. You can't get out without going past them. And they only let you past if you need to go to the bathroom, or if you're hurt or sick and need to go to the nurse.

I didn't want to lie. But I also didn't want Cosmo to be alone. "Excuse me," I said to Mrs. Fisher. "Can I go to the bathroom?"

"*May* you," she said.

"What?"

"I'm certain you *can* go to the bathroom," Mrs. Fisher said. "But you're asking permission about whether you *may* go, right?"

"Right."

"Yes, you may—just as soon as one of your friends comes back with the pass."

"Oh," I said. "Okay."

I stood there waiting. It took a long time. Finally, Claire pushed open the door. She handed the pass back to Mrs. Fisher. "I couldn't get the sink to turn off," Claire said.

"Is the water leaking onto the floor?" Mr. Berry asked.

"Not yet," Claire said. "I put some paper towels on the floor just in case—don't you think that makes me a good citizen?"

"Certainly," Mr. Berry said.

Our principal, Mr. Goldblatt, started a good citizen program in our school. If you do good citizen things, you might get picked to do the morning announcements on the loud speaker.

"Will you tell Mr. Goldblatt?" Claire asked.

"Uh, sure," Mr. Berry said.

"Excuse me," I said. "Can I have the bathroom pass now?"

"You don't need it," Mrs. Fisher said. "I'm coming with you."

Uh oh. If Mrs. Fisher came with me, I wouldn't be able to skip going to the bathroom and really go back to my classroom! "I can go by myself," I said.

"I'm sure you can," she said. "But I need to check out that sink. Let's go, shall we?"

We walked down the hall to the bathroom. I went into one of the stalls and pretended to go while Mrs. Fisher fixed the sink. I counted to twenty, then I flushed.

When I came out, Mrs. Fisher was standing there. She waited for me to wash my hands, in case I couldn't turn the faucet off. But I could. It wasn't a problem at all. It was like Claire made it all up.

The rest of recess passed by suuuuuper slooooowly. Finally, the bell rang. I was the first to line up to go back to class. I walked so quickly down the hallway that Ms. Serrato had to tell me to slow down. We got back to the classroom, and I speed-walked to my cubby in the back.

Something was wrong. I could tell right away. I'd only left my backpack open this much:

Now, it was open all the way. My heart was suddenly pounding. My hands felt sticky. I was afraid to look inside my backpack. And when I did . . . Cosmo was gone!

"AHHHHH!" I cried out.

Ms. Serrato ran to me. "Piper, what happened? Are you sick? Are you hurt?"

I shook my head. For a couple of seconds, I couldn't even find the words to tell her. I just pointed at my backpack.

"What?" she asked.

"My very important thing is MISSING!" I cried.

MR. GOLDBLATT

"I knew I should've taken my backpack to lunch with me!" I said.

"Sometimes we think something is missing, but really we've just misplaced it," Ms. Serrato said.

"I didn't misplace anything!" I cried. "I think Claire stole it!"

"What are you blaming me for?" Claire said.

"You were the one who wanted to know what I had in my backpack," I said. "Everyone else was minding their own business."

"I know you're upset, Piper," Ms. Serrato said. "But it's not okay to accuse Claire. She walked out of this classroom at the same time you did."

"She went to the bathroom during indoor recess," I said. "And she took a really long time in there—enough time to come all the way back here and open my backpack."

"I was trying to turn the sink off," Claire said.

"I went to the bathroom right after you and I turned the sink off no problem," I said.

"Now, now," Ms. Serrato said. "Why don't you tell us what's missing, and we can all help you look for it—"

"I don't help people who call me a liar," Claire said.

"Prove you're not a liar," I said. "Let me see inside your backpack."

"You can't look in my backpack," Claire said.

"That proves that you *are* a liar!"

"It doesn't prove anything except that you're completely weird!" Claire said. "There wasn't even anything in there except some empty lunch containers and a dust rag."

"It was a blankie, and that proves you DID go into my backpack!"

"Claire, is that true?" Ms. Serrato asked.

Before Claire could answer, I grabbed her backpack out of her cubby. "Hey!" he said. She grabbed it back from

me, and there was a *riiiiiiiiiiip* sound. "She broke it! She broke my backpack!"

It fell to the ground. Some pencils, an eraser, and her scooter helmet tumbled out.

But no Cosmo.

"Piper, Claire, I think you both need to take a trip to Mr. Goldblatt," Ms. Serrato said.

"But I have my Show and Tell about my dog, Buddy, all ready to go!" Claire said.

"And I didn't rip her backpack on purpose," I said. "I only did it because she stole something out of mine."

"I already told you there wasn't anything in yours."

"Theo, will you walk them to the principal's office?" Ms. Serrato asked.

"Sure," Theo said.

Ms. Serrato wrote a note to Mr. Goldblatt and handed it to Theo.

I guess she didn't trust Claire or me to deliver it. We walked down the hall. Claire was grumbling about missing Show and Tell. But who cares about missing Show and Tell when you're missing your pet? I'd wanted a pet my whole life. Now I finally had one, and he was already gone.

I didn't believe that Claire didn't find him in my backpack. But if she didn't put him in *her* backpack, then where was he? I hoped wherever he was, it wasn't too dark and scary and there were breathing holes. Was he alive right now, or back to being plain slime? If he was alive, he must be so scared. Poor little Cosmo. What if I never saw him again?

Tears pricked behind my eyes. I bit my lip to keep from crying in front of Claire.

We got to the principal's office. Theo gave the note to Mrs. Carrion, Mr. Goldblatt's assistant. "You can go back to class now," Mrs. Carrion told him. "You two sit right there," she said, pointing to the bench right outside Mr. Goldblatt's office. "He'll call you in soon."

I could hear Mr. Goldblatt on the phone on the other side of the wall. He has the kind of voice that's loud even when he's just regular talking. It makes him even scarier. There is a big clock on the wall above Mrs. Carrion's desk, and I watched the minutes tick by.

"It's your fault that we're missing *all* of Show and Tell," Claire whispered to me.

A few minutes passed. I heard Mr. Goldblatt say, "All right, Bill. Call me back when you have the answer on that."

Something buzzed on Mrs. Carrion's desk. "Piper, Claire, you may go in now," she said.

Mr. Goldblatt was sitting behind a large wooden desk. He's really tall, so even when he's sitting down, he's taller than most kids. Claire and I each took a seat in the chairs in front of him. "Tell me what happened, girls," he said.

His voice was so loud that it echoed. For a second, I was quiet and so was

Claire. Then we both started talking at the same time.

"She went into my backpack," I said.

"She called me a liar," Claire said.

"She *was* a liar," I said.

"And she ripped my backpack," Claire said.

Mr. Goldblatt held up his hand. It was as big as a basketball. "One at a time," he boomed. "Claire, what happened?"

"We got back to our class after recess. Piper said I'd stolen something out of her backpack. But I didn't."

"What was in your backpack, Piper?" Mr. Goldblatt asked.

"Uh . . . it was slime. I made it last night."

"Slime?" Claire asked. "You're being this weird about homemade slime?"

My cheeks burned. "It was special," I said. "I made the slime into a pet. He's purple all over, with a rounded head, a teeny mouth, and big eyes. He's about

113

this big." I held up my hands to show the size of a kitten. "And he's just the cutest thing I've ever seen."

"You were *talking* to the slime like it was alive," Claire said. "Weirdo."

"I didn't let anyone see it," I told Mr. Goldblatt. "But Claire kept asking me about it, and then she took a long time going to the bathroom at lunch. She pretended the sink was broken, but really she went into my backpack."

"I didn't take anything out of it," she said.

"Now she's lying again."

"I'm not! I swear on my dog Buddy's life that I'm not!"

Mr. Goldblatt's phone rang and he held up his hand again. "Hello?" he said into the phone. "Oh, Bill. Thanks for getting back to me so quickly . . . uh huh . . . uh huh . . . hang on, please." He put his hand over the mouthpiece and looked down at us. "Girls, I have to deal with the order for a new smartboard in the auditorium," he said. "Piper, I'm sorry you lost your slime. But Claire says she didn't take it, and I believe her."

"Is Piper going to be punished for saying I did something when I didn't?" Claire asked.

"Yes," Mr. Goldblatt said.

"What?" I asked at the same time that Claire said, "Good."

I felt the tears pricking again. First, I got punished at home. Now I was going to be punished at school.

Worst of all, Cosmo was still missing.

"You're both going to be punished," Mr. Goldblatt said. "We don't falsely accuse people at this school, Piper. But we don't touch other people's property either, Claire. So, this afternoon, you two are going to stay an extra half hour to help Mr. Leon sweep the third-grade classrooms."

Mr. Leon is the janitor at school.

"But I was a good citizen at lunch!" Claire said. "I put paper towels down so the floor wouldn't get too wet."

"It's our job to be good citizens all day long, every day," Mr. Goldblatt said. "Mrs. Carrion will take care of letting your parents know what's happening. Go on, now. I need to finish this phone call." He uncovered the mouthpiece. "Bill, I'm back . . . uh huh . . . uh huh."

He waved one of his giant hands at us to let us know we were supposed to walk out the door, and so we did.

THE CLEAN TEAM

Mrs. Carrion gave us a note to bring to Ms. Serrato. By the time we got back to class, Show and Tell was over.

Not that I cared. The only thing that I cared about was Cosmo. I couldn't concentrate on any of the afternoon lessons. I pictured Cosmo escaping from wherever Claire had hidden him and wandering through the halls of our school looking for me. He couldn't talk, so he couldn't ask anyone how to find me. And even if he *could* talk, he turned back to slime whenever anyone saw him—besides me. Kids could run into the halls and squish him to death under their shoes.

The bell rang at the end of the day. Everyone was dismissed, except for Claire and me. We had to wait for Mr. Leon. Ms. Serrato sat at her desk and did paperwork. Claire and I sat next to each other at our Table B seats.

Cosmo, Cosmo, where are you? I thought.

"Stop staring at me," Claire said.

"I'm not staring."

"Yes, you are."

"No, I'm not."

"That's enough," Ms. Serrato said.

"Knock, knock," a voice called from the doorway.

"Hey there, Mr. Leon," Ms. Serrato said. "Looks like you have some helpers today." She picked up her bag. "Have a good afternoon, girls," she told us. "Tomorrow is a new day."

"All right, Clean Team!" Mr. Leon said. "You ready to make some moves?"

"Yeah," Claire and I mumbled.

Mr. Leon cupped a hand to his ear.

"I said, YOU READY TO MAKE SOME MOVES?"

"Yeah," we said a little bit louder.

"Hmm," Mr. Leon said. "Call me crazy, but I don't think you two are happy to be hanging out with me this afternoon."

"I'm sorry," I told Mr. Leon. "It's not because of you. Something important to me is missing. That's why I'm unhappy."

"It's just slime," Claire said, rolling her eyes. "And *I'm* unhappy because Piper thinks it's my fault, but it's not."

"Are there any distinguishing characteristics about the missing slime?" Mr. Leon asked.

"Oh yeah," I said. "It's purple and as big as a kitten, but with a rounded head, big eyes, a teeny mouth, and little arms that are just long enough for cuddling."

Claire rolled her eyes again.

"Have you seen anything like it?" I asked.

"I don't believe I have," Mr. Leon said. "But I'll keep an eye out now. Lucky for you, I happen to know the best method for finding lost things."

"What?"

"Cleaning!" he said. He turned to Claire. "And even if it's not your fault that Piper's slime is missing, helping to find it would be a good citizen thing to do."

"Yeah, but it's not like I'll get to make morning announcements or anything," she said.

"Hey, you never know," Mr. Leon said. "So, what do you say—can we get started?"

"Fine," Claire said.

"Okay," I said.

"Fist bump!" Mr. Leon said. He held out a fist, and we both bumped it. "Now, on to Mrs. Wade's classroom."

"Why don't we start right where we are?" Claire asked.

"I always start with Mrs. Wade's room," Mr. Leon said. "You know why?"

"Why?"

"Because she teaches in Classroom 3A, and A comes before B in the alphabet. Let's make some moves!"

He bopped his head as he crossed the hall. Claire and I just regular-walked. Mrs. Wade had put all her students' names up on the board on sunshine-shaped construction paper. In our classroom, our names are on diamonds. Mrs. Wade's room also had the desks set up in rows. Ms. Serrato had pushed our desks together to make Table A and Table B.

Mr. Leon told us to lift the chairs onto the desks. That way, it'd be easier to sweep under them. I checked under every single desk, looking for Cosmo. But I didn't find him.

When all the chairs were lifted, Mr. Leon did the sweeping. Claire and I took turns holding the dustpan.

"Good job, clean team," Mr. Leon said. "Now on to 3B. Let's make some moves!"

Back in our classroom, we lifted the chairs again. I looked for Cosmo under every desk—especially Claire's desk. But he wasn't there.

"I need a break," Claire said after the last chair was lifted. She leaned against the back cabinets, accidentally knocking Mr. Swimmers' fish flakes onto the floor. "Uh oh."

"No biggie," Mr. Leon said. "That's what the broom is for. Can you bring over the dustpan?"

"I don't have it," Claire said.

"Me neither," I said.

"You used it last," she said.

"No, you did."

"No, *YOU* . . . oh, maybe I did," she said. "But that means it was your turn to remember to bring it back here."

Mr. Leon started to laugh.

"What's so funny?" Claire asked.

"Nothing at all," Mr. Leon said. "You two take a break. I'll grab the dustpan."

He went across the hall. I scooped up a handful of fish flakes. "Why are you doing that?" she asked. "Mr. Leon said he'd sweep it up."

"Just getting a head start," I said.

"You're only doing that to be a better good citizen."

"No, I'm not."

"Yes, you are." She slid off the back cabinets, scooped up a giant handful of fish flakes, and ran toward the garbage can next to Ms. Serrato's desk. "AHHHH!" she gasped. She took a couple steps backward and knocked into the white board. The flakes she was holding fell to the ground.

"What happened?" I asked.

"There's something . . . there's something ALIVE in the garbage can!"

My heart started thumping. I raced over.

Could it be him?

Please, please, let it be him.

"COSMO!" I cried.

ALMOST A
HAPPY ENDING

He was sitting on top of a bunch of crumpled papers. I scooped him up and cuddled him close. "I was so, so worried about you!" I said. "How did you end up in there?"

Cosmo didn't answer. He just made his good Cosmo sounds. There was a rubber band stuck to his head, and a tissue stuck to his body. I pulled them off and brushed away the Oreo crumbs around his mouth.

"You ate my lunch, didn't you?" I said.

Cosmo gurgled.

"I'm sorry. I didn't realize you'd need food, since you're slime. But of course you do, because anything that's alive needs food—no matter what it's made of!"

"That's . . . that's the slime you made?" Claire asked.

I nodded. "It is."

"But how is it . . . what is it . . . am I dreaming?"

"He started out as plain slime," I said. "I sculpted him into a pet. Then some space dust fell on him. That's when he came to life."

"Wow," Claire said. "ICBI."

"Huh?"

"I can't believe it," she said.

"He turned back to slime in front of my parents," I said. "I thought that meant I was the only one he could come alive for. But . . . "

"But he's alive for me, too," Claire said.

I nodded. "Maybe he can be alive for kids but not adults."

"Maybe," Claire said. "You're right about one thing—he's the cutest thing

I've ever seen. Except for Buddy, that is.
Is it okay if I pet him?"

"Sure," I said. "Claire, let me introduce
you to Cosmo. Cosmo, this is Claire."

Claire reached out her hand and
ran her fingers across Cosmo's soft,

slimy back. "I didn't take him out of your backpack, Piper," Claire said. "I swear. I hope you believe me."

"I believe you," I said. "I left it open a little bit, so he could breathe. I think maybe he opened it up all the way himself and climbed out to look for me."

"How do you think he ended up in the garbage can?"

"Maybe Ms. Serrato came into the room and thought that he was just plain slime, so she threw him away."

"Poor Cosmo," Claire said.

"Please don't tell anyone about him," I said. "I tried to tell my mom this morning. He looked like regular slime to her, so that's what she thought he was. I think he's supposed to be a secret."

"I won't tell," Claire said. "I promise."

"I'm going to teach him tricks, like you taught Buddy," I said. "He already knows how to sit—sort of. If I push his butt down, he sits. What else can Buddy do?"

"Oh, lots of things," Claire said. "He can fetch balls, and lie down, and hold a paw for a shake."

"You want to learn all that, Cosmo?" I asked.

He made his gurgle sounds.

"Girls!" Mr. Leon said. Claire and I both jumped. "Didn't mean to scare you," he said. "And I didn't mean to take so long. I needed to help find a missing mop. How are you guys doing?"

"We're all good," Claire said. "Everything is totally normal."

"Better than normal," I said. "You found the mop, and I found my slime!"

"That's it right there?" Mr. Leon asked.

"Yep." Cosmo had turned back to plain slime in my arms, but he still looked cute to me.

"That's the best-looking slime I've ever seen," Mr. Leon said. "I'm glad you found it."

"Actually, Claire found it," I said.

"But Piper made it," Claire said. "If she didn't make it, there wouldn't have been anything to find."

"That's surely true," Mr. Leon said. "Way to go, Clean Team. I love a happy ending."

"ALMOST happy ending," I said. "We still need to sweep this room."

"You two ready to make some moves with the dustpan?" Mr. Leon asked.

"Yes!" Claire and I said.

13

OH NO, GRANDMA!

About an hour later, I was back at home. Dad was in his office, still working on the tough section of his book. He told me I had to play alone. That was fine with me, because I wasn't actually alone. I'd never have to play alone again. I had Cosmo.

I sat down on my bedroom floor and patted the rug beside me.

"C'mere, Cosmo," I said. "Sit."

He sat! All by himself!

"Oh, good boy," I said. "Now I'm going to teach you to play fetch, like Claire's dog, Buddy." I held up a tennis ball. "When I roll this across the room, you go get it and bring it back, okay?"

Cosmo gurgled, which I took as a yes.

"Here we go," I said. I rolled the ball. "Get it, boy!"

Cosmo hopped after the ball, scooped it up, and brought it back.

"You're a natural at fetching," I told him. "Let's play again."

I rolled the ball. Cosmo took a couple of steps toward it. But then he seemed to change his mind about fetching. He turned around and hopped into my lap.

"Oh, you just want to snuggle?" I asked. "Well, that's okay, too. Let's snuggle. We can do tricks later. You've had a long day."

I hugged Cosmo in my lap. He felt so cozy. I didn't care about being allergic anymore. Even if I wasn't allergic to anything, and I could have whatever pet I wanted out of all the pets in the whole wide world, I'd still pick Cosmo.

Dad pushed open the door, and Cosmo turned back to regular slime. "Hey, there

Piper," he said. "You wrote to Grandma Sadie last night, didn't you?"

"Yep. I thanked her for my space dust. It was actually a much better present than I thought, just so you know."

"Why's that?" he asked.

"Oh, no reason," I said.

"Hmm . . . well, you didn't by any chance get an email back from your grandma, did you?"

"I haven't checked yet."

"Let's check now," Dad said.

"Okay," I said.

I scooped up Cosmo—he was just a slime blob in front of Dad, but I still wanted to keep him near me. We walked down the hall to Dad's office. Dad pulled out the desk chair in front of his computer so I could sit down and log on. I typed in my email address and password.

"Anything from Grandma Sadie?" he asked.

"No, not yet," I said. "But I'm going to write her another email anyway. I have something important to tell her."

"What?"

"It's private," I said.

It was about Cosmo, of course. I wanted her to know what the space dust did to my slime and give her an extra-big thank you. But I didn't want Dad to see because I knew he wouldn't understand.

Dad was still standing right next to me. "That means I need privacy," I told him.

"Oh, right. Of course," he said, and he took a step back. But his voice sounded funny. He looked funny, too. His forehead was all scrunched up, the way it gets when he's worried about something.

"Is something wrong?" I asked.

"Oh, it's probably nothing," Dad said. "You know your grandmother. She goes off on adventures all the time. But . . . "

"But what?"

"Mom got a call from Grandma Sadie's boss at AstroBlast Explorers," he said. "She was supposed to blast off on a

144

new trip this morning. She's probably fine. But she didn't come in, and they don't know where she is."

"They don't know where she is?" I repeated, and Dad nodded. "You mean she's *missing*?" I asked.

"I'm afraid so," he said.

"Oh no, Grandma Sadie!" I cried.

My pet Slime

More to Explore

Piper Maclane's Secret Slime Recipe

Hey, it's me, Piper Maclane. I'm going to share my favorite slime recipe with you. You should have your parents help you make it so that you don't get in trouble the way I did. You only need three ingredients:

1. **A 6-ounce bottle of white or clear school glue**

2. **½ teaspoon baking soda**

3. **1½ tablespoons contact lens solution that includes boric acid and sodium borate**

First, squeeze the whole bottle of glue into a bowl. Next, add the baking soda and mix it up.

Want your slime to be stretchier? Add a few tablespoons of water.

After that, slowly mix in the contact lens solution.

You can also add food coloring or glitter to make your slime more colorful or sparkly! Mix it up with your hands until it's smooth and stretchy.

Your slime might not come to life the way that Cosmo did, but you'll have a lot of fun making it!

Real-Life Slime

Cosmo might be a fictional character, but guess what? Scientists in France have discovered a slime that can do tricks in REAL life! Its name is "Physarum Polycephalum." Let's call it P. Slime for short.

P. Slime doesn't have a brain, so it can't be taught how to sit or fetch a ball, or anything like that. But it can figure out how to slink around and find food.

When the scientists put barriers in between P. Slime and its food, the slime worked out a way around the barrier to get what it wanted. Sometimes it seemed to be a little bit scared, and it wouldn't move. But then it learned not to be scared of the barrier anymore.

That's a pretty good lesson—to gather up your courage and face your fears. Who knew slime would be such a great teacher?

Maybe one day scientists will discover a slime that's brave as well as cute and cuddly like Cosmo.

In the meantime, there will be plenty
of Cosmo and Piper adventures to enjoy!

About the Author

Courtney Sheinmel is a chocolate lover, a mac-and-cheese expert, and the author of over twenty highly celebrated books for kids and teens, including the middle grade series *The Kindness Club*, and the young readers' series *Stella Batts* and *Magic on the Map*. She lives in New York City.

About the Illustrator

Renée Kurilla has illustrated many books for kids. She lives just south of Boston with her husband, daughter, and a plump orange cat who springs to life the moment everyone else falls asleep. Renée loves drawing nature, animals, and projects that require a bit of research. When she is not drawing, she is likely to be found plucking at her ukulele or gluing together tiny dollhouse miniatures.

My Pet Slime

Andrews McMeel Publishing
a division of Andrews McMeel Universal
1130 Walnut Street, Kansas City, Missouri 64106

www.andrewsmcmeel.com

Epic! Creations, Inc.
702 Marshall Street, Suite 280, Redwood, California 94063

www.getepic.com

20 21 22 23 24 SDB 10 9 8 7 6 5 4 3 2 1

Paperback ISBN: 978-1-5248-5520-8
Hardback ISBN: 978-1-5248-5545-1

Library of Congress Control Number: 2019941824

Design by Ariana Abud and Wendy Gable
Slime mold photograph by Simia Attentive,
licensed from Shutterstock

Made by:
King Yip (Dongguan) Printing & Packaging Factory Ltd.
Address and location of production:
Daning Administrative District, Humen Town
Dongguan Guangdong, China 523930
1st Printing — 6/1/20

ATTENTION: SCHOOLS AND BUSINESSES
Andrews McMeel books are available at quantity
discounts with bulk purchase for educational, business,
or sales promotional use. For information, please
e-mail the Andrews McMeel Publishing Special Sales
Department: specialsales@amuniversal.com.

Don't miss Cosmo and Piper's next adventure

Cosmo to the Rescue